For Krystyna
—L.J.

For Lucy & Sophie
—C.J.C.

LITTLE TIGER PRESS
N16 W23390 Stoneridge Drive, Waukesha, WI 53188
First published in the United States 1999
Originally published in Great Britain 1999 by
Little Tiger Press, an imprint of Magi Publications, London
Text © 1999 Linda Jennings · Illustrations © 1999 Caroline Jayne Church
CIP Data is available · First American Edition
Printed in Singapore · All rights reserved · ISBN 1-888444-62-2
1 3 5 7 9 10 8 6 4 2

Nine Naughty Kittens

by Linda Jennings & Caroline Jayne Church

One
wobbly kitten,
after something
new. . . .

Kitten meets
another one,
and then there
are . . .

Two tiny
kittens,
what can
they see?

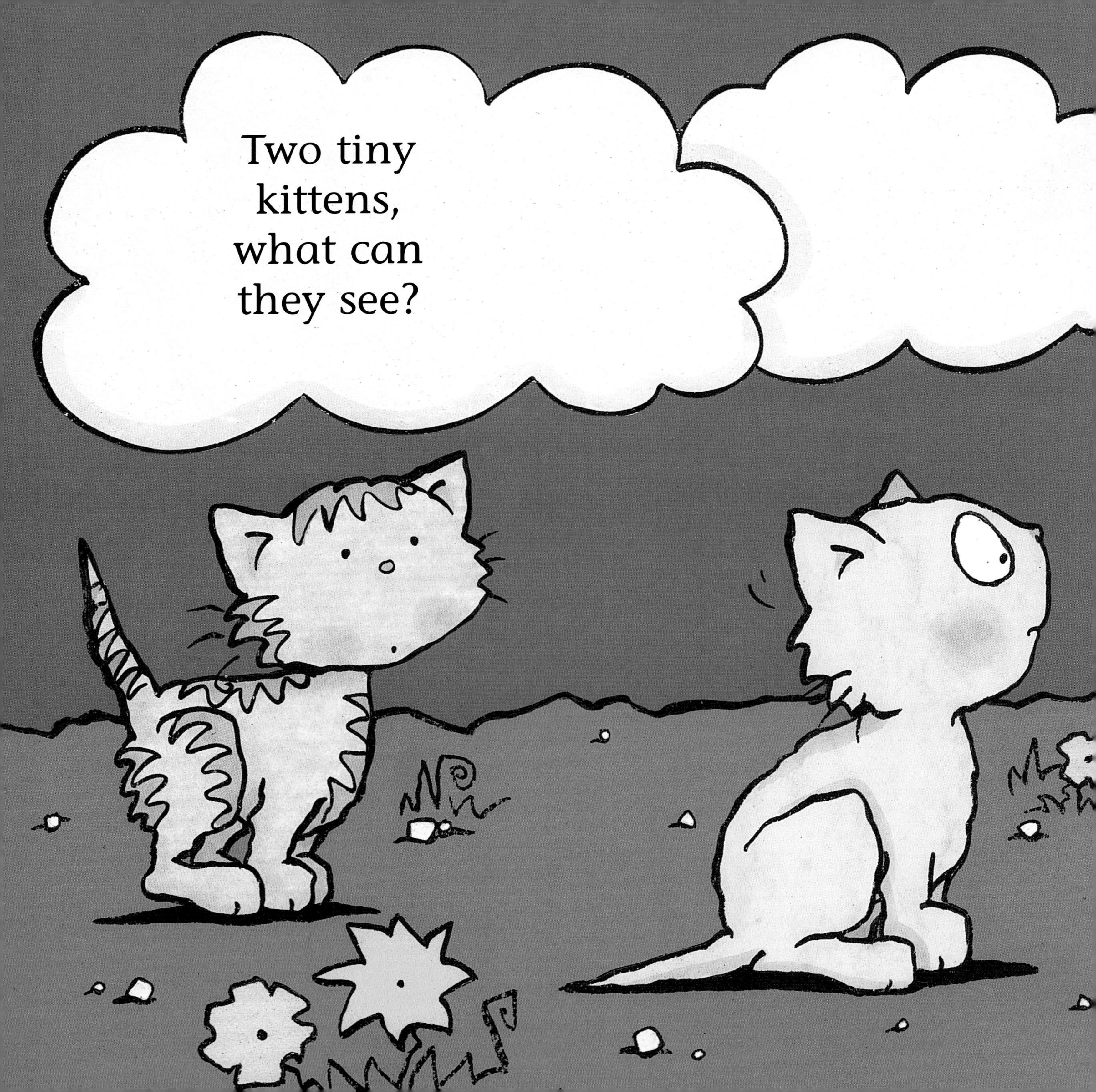

Kittens find their brother, and then there are . . .

Three frightened kittens, peeping round the door. . . .

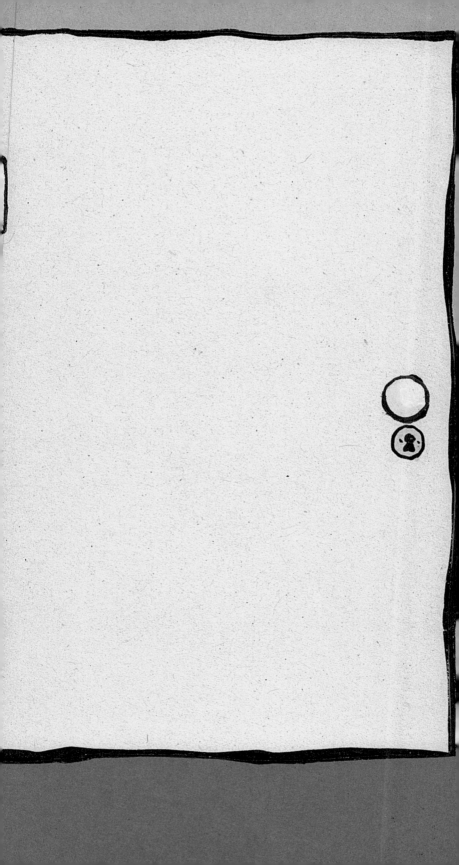

"Boo!" says
little Ginger,
and then there
are . . .

Four
frisky kittens,
glad to be
alive. . . .

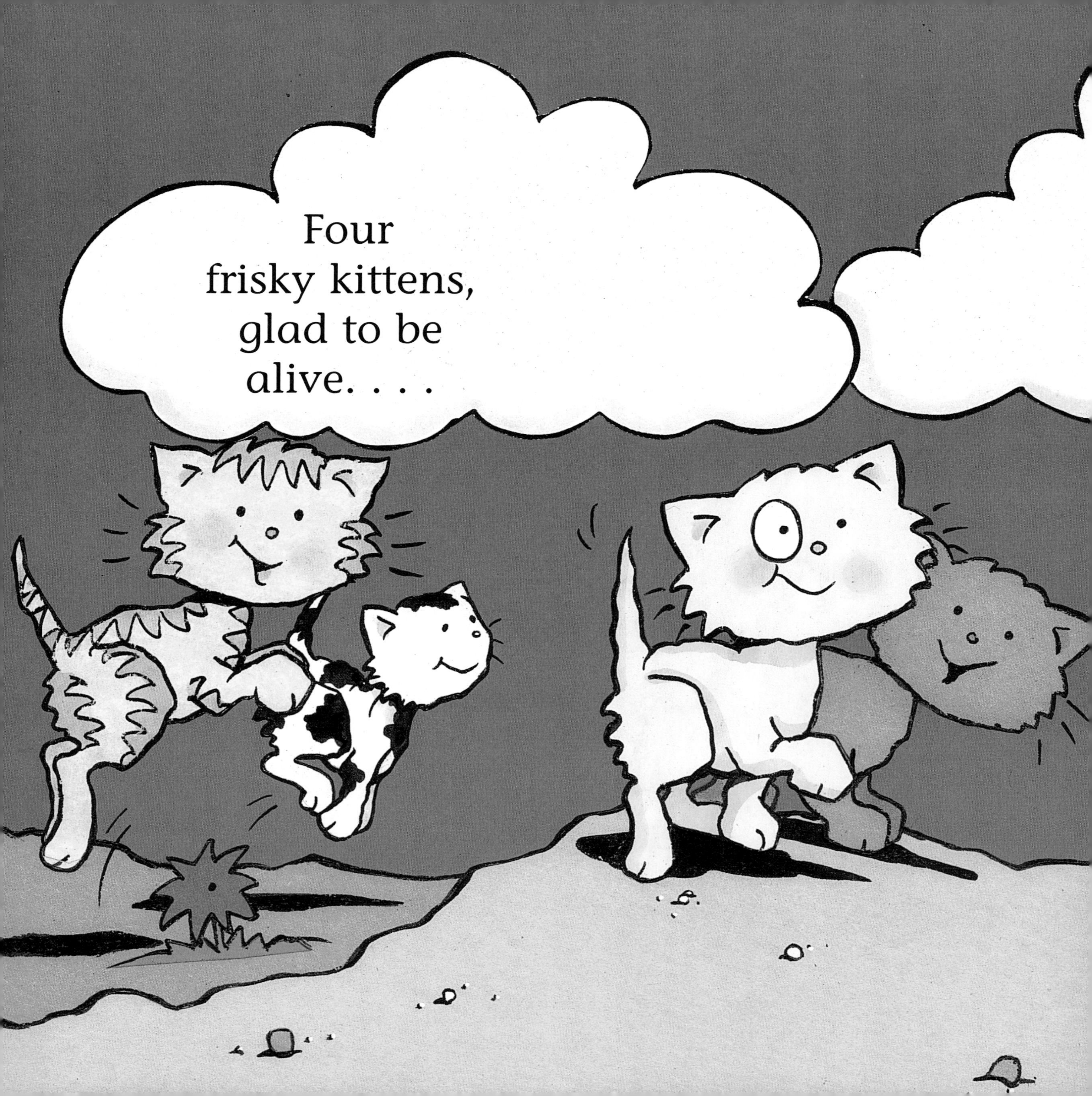

skip to meet
another one,
and then
there are . . .

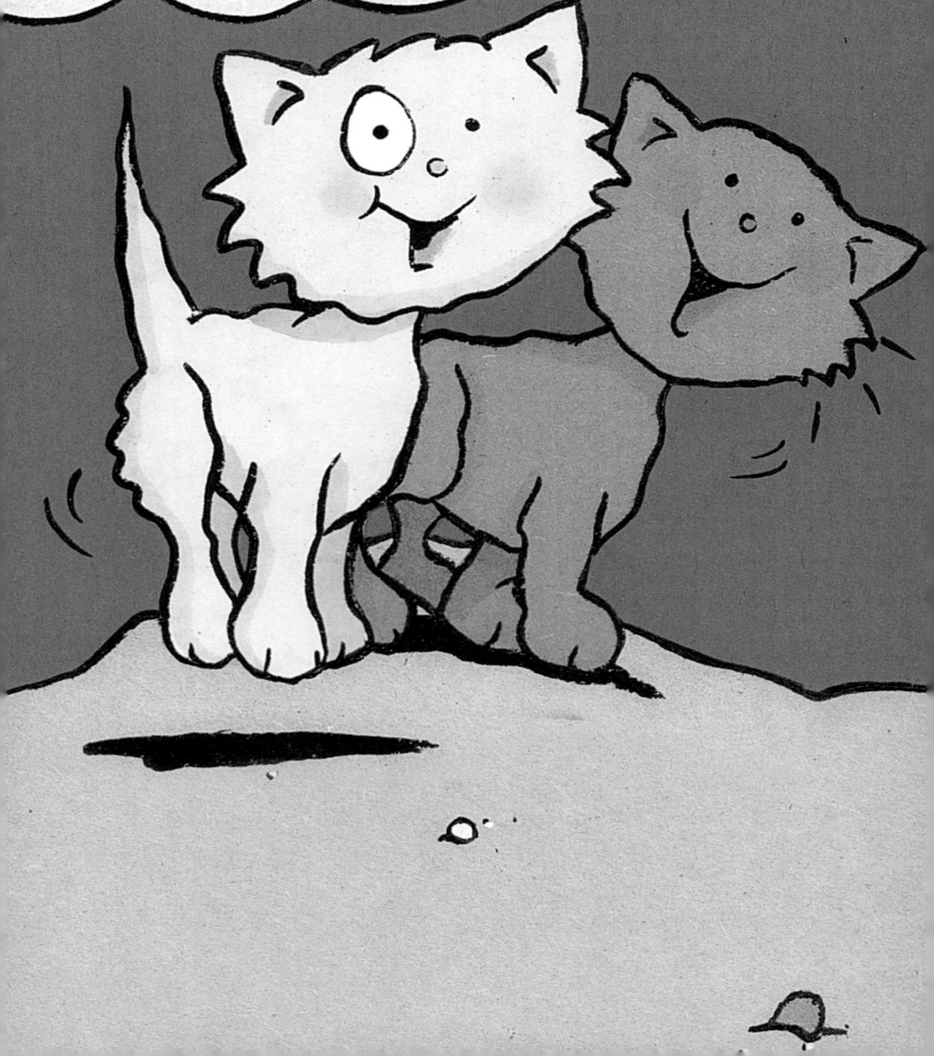

Five furry
kittens
find a
pile of
sticks. . . .

Jasper's
sleeping
under them,
and then
there are . . .

six

Six sniffing
kittens
find a fishy
heaven. . . .

but their sister
got there first,
and then there
are . . .

Seven

Seven silly
kittens try
to climb a
gate. . . .

jump upon
another kitten,
then there
are . . .

Eight
eager kittens,
walking in a
line. . . .

Nine naughty kittens find a cozy den. . . .

"Come to me," says Mother Cat, and then there are . . .

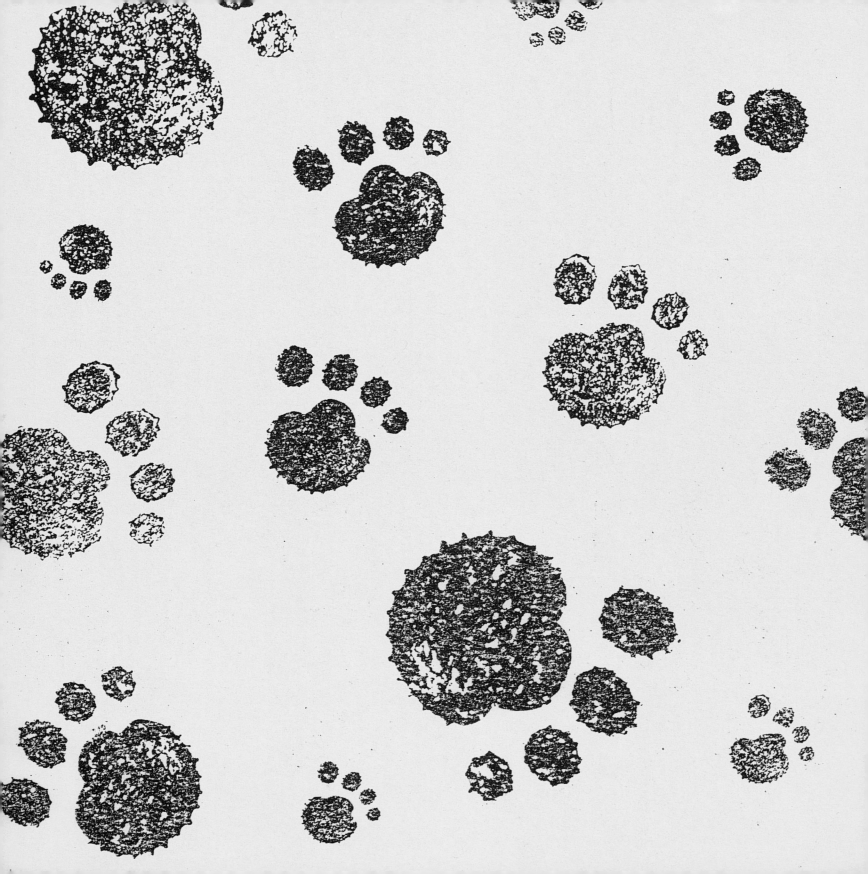